My Name Is
Saajin Singh

Written by
Kuljinder Kaur Brar

Illustrated by
Samrath Kaur

annick
press
toronto · berkeley

Saajin (Sah-jin) loved his name.
He saw it in the clouds.

He wrote it with his cereal.

He even sang it in the tub.

He loved the way it looked.
He loved the way it tasted.
And he loved the way it sounded.

On the first day of school, Saajin wore his favorite t-shirt. He wore his favorite shoes. He even wore his favorite food.

"Yay, school!" exclaimed Saajin. "I'm going to make so many new friends!"

"I'm sure you will." Dad smiled and gave him a big hug.

Everything felt right, until Mrs. Wilson took attendance.

"When I call your name, your job is to say 'here' and raise your hand, so I know who came to school today."

"Sarah?"

"Here!"

"Matthew?"

"Here!"

"Kelly?"

"Here!"

"Eric?"

"Here!"

Mrs. Wilson took a long pause
and raised her eyebrow.
"Say-jin?"
There was no response.

SAY-JIN?

"Um . . . Say-jin?" repeated Mrs. Wilson.

Saajin looked around. His name hadn't been called yet.

"Say-jin Singh," said Mrs. Wilson, as she continued to look around the room.

Saajin knew that was his last name. But the first name didn't sound right. He didn't like the sound of that name.

"Everyone please listen carefully. Is there a Say-jin Singh who is here today?"

Saajin went red in his cheeks, shrugged his shoulders, and raised his hand, "Here."

Mrs. Wilson finished off the rest of the attendance and Saajin didn't hear any other name that sounded familiar, so he knew he made the right choice by raising his hand.

"Hi Say-jin, do you want to play tag?"
Kelly asked later that morning at recess.

Saajin paused and nodded his head.

That must be how people say my name when I leave the house, he thought to himself.

From that day on, Mrs. Wilson and all of Saajin's friends knew him as Say-jin.

And his name started to feel . . . different.

It didn't look right when he wrote it with his favorite crayon.

It didn't taste as sweet
when he ate his jalebi.

And it didn't sound right when
he whispered it to his dog.

Sometimes hearing his
friends say Say-jin made
Saajin's stomach feel funny.

And sometimes,
only sometimes, it
made him feel sad.

One day after school, Saajin noticed new neighbors moving in next door. Mom and Dad thought it would be a good idea to go over and make them feel welcome.

"Hi," said Saajin, as he lowered his head and spoke quietly.
"My name is Say-jin Singh."
His name sounded like a frog was stuck in his throat.

"Hi, I'm Christopher Thompson," said the boy proudly.
"But I like it when people call me Chris."

Saajin liked Chris. He liked how they both loved dinosaurs.
He liked how they both had a dog as a best friend.
He even liked how they both had the same shoes.

Saajin told Chris about the school playground and how long and twisty the slide was. He even told him about the big puddle that everyone loved to jump in.

Saajin couldn't wait to show Chris around the school.

Dinnertime was quiet that night.

"Saajin," asked Dad finally, "I'm wondering why you called yourself Say-jin when we met with our new neighbors."

"My name is Say-jin, Dad," answered Saajin.
"That's my name when I leave the house."

"What do you mean?" questioned Mom.

"Mrs. Wilson calls me Say-jin. Everyone at school calls me Say-jin. I don't like the way it sounds, but that's how people say it. My name at home is Sah-jin, but when I leave the house, it's Say-jin."

"Hmm . . . how would you like people to say your name?" asked Dad.

Saajin quickly replied, "I like it when people call me Sah-jin . . . but Mrs. Wilson said my name is Say-jin and Mrs. Wilson knows everything, because she's the teacher . . . and grown-ups don't make mistakes!"

"Remember the time Dad forgot his keys in the car and was locked out? That was a mistake," said Mom.

"Or the time Mom lost her phone in the park. That was also a mistake." Dad laughed.

Saajin couldn't believe it.

He had made lots of mistakes in his life, like going down the hill too fast on his bike and not being able to stop.

Or the time he got so carried away coloring in his book
that he somehow ended up coloring on the walls.

He didn't realize that grown-ups could make mistakes too . . .

"Saajin, do you remember what your name means in Punjabi?" asked Dad.

Saajin nodded. It meant "loving friend."

It was the reason why he loved his name so much.
He was everyone's loving friend and proud of it.

"When you don't pronounce it as 'Sah-jin,'
it loses its meaning."

Saajin was surprised to hear this.

He went to bed that night with a lot to think about.

The next morning, Saajin
wore his favorite jacket.
He wore his favorite socks.
He even wore his favorite drink.

The bell rang and Mrs. Wilson was ready to take the attendance.

"Sarah?"

"Here!"

"Matthew?"

"Here!"

"Kelly?"

"Here!"

"Eric?"

"Here!"

"Say-jin?"

SAY-JIN?

Good Morning!
- Attendance
- Calend
- Literacy
- Recess
- Math
- Lunch
- Story Cent
- Dis

"Actually, Mrs. Wilson, my name is Sah-jin.
It means 'loving friend' in Punjabi," explained Saajin.

"Oh dear, Sah-jin, I'm so sorry I said your name wrong. I should have asked you how to pronounce it. And that's such a beautiful meaning," apologized Mrs. Wilson. "Thank you for letting me know."

"It's okay, Mrs. Wilson," smiled Saajin. "Everyone makes mistakes . . . even grown-ups."

That afternoon, Saajin happily corrected his friends, and even grown-ups, when they mispronounced his name.

Saajin loved his name.
He saw it in the stars.
He wrote it with his roti.

He even sang it in the car.

He loved the way it looked.
He loved the way it tasted.
But most of all, he loved the way it sounded.

It is common practice for Sikhs to go to the temple, also known as the Gurdwara, for a naming ceremony called Naam Karan.

The Sikh holy book, the Guru Granth Sahib, is opened to a random page and a hymn, Hukam, is read aloud.

The hymns in the Guru Granth Sahib are written in Gurmukhi, an alphabet of 35 letters. The first letter of the first word from the Hukam determines the first letter of the baby's name.

Many Sikh names, like Saajin's, have meaning behind them.

For my son, Saajin, who made me both a
mom and an author.
—K. B.

For my brother, Makhlook Singh.
—S. K.

Kuljinder Kaur Brar is an elementary teacher. She lives
in Abbotsford, British Columbia, and this is her first book.
She has a son named Saajin who inspired the story.

Samrath Kaur is an illustrator and background painter,
and this is his first book. He lives in Boston.

© 2022 Kuljinder Kaur Brar (text)
© 2022 Samrath Kaur (illustrations)

Cover art by Samrath Kaur, designed by Paul Covello
Interior designed by Paul Covello
Edited by Gayna Theophilus

Annick Press Ltd.

We acknowledge the support of the Canada Council for the Arts and the
Ontario Arts Council, and the participation of the Government of Canada/la
participation du gouvernement du Canada for our publishing activities.

ONTARIO ARTS COUNCIL
CONSEIL DES ARTS DE L'ONTARIO
an Ontario government agency
un organisme du gouvernement de l'Ontario

Library and Archives Canada Cataloguing in Publication

Title: My name is Saajin Singh / written by Kuljinder Kaur Brar ; illustrated by Samrath Kaur
Names: Brar, Kuljinder Kaur, author. | Kaur, Samrath, illustrator
Identifiers: Canadiana (print) 20220171181 | Canadiana (ebook) 2022017119X | ISBN 9781773217055
(hardcover) | ISBN 9781773217079 (HTML) | ISBN 9781773217093 (PDF)
Classification: LCC PS8603.R3616 M92 2022 | DDC jC813/.6—dc23

Published in the U.S.A. by Annick Press (U.S.) Ltd.
Distributed in Canada by University of Toronto Press.
Distributed in the U.S.A. by Publishers Group West.

Printed in China

annickpress.com
kuljinderwrites.com
smrth.net

Also available as an e-book. Please visit annickpress.com/ebooks for more details.